STARSHIP TROOPERS

™

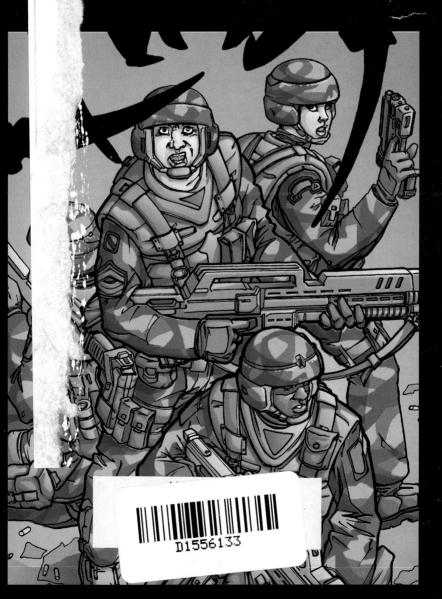

STARSHIP TROOPERS
ISBN 1 85286 886 4

Published by Titan Books Ltd
42 - 44 Dolben St
London SE1 0UP

Originally published in single magazine form by Dark Horse Comics as Starship Troopers: Insect Touch 1–3,
Starship Troopers: Brute Creations, and Starship Troopers 1–2.

British Library Cataloguing-In-Publication data. A catalogue record for this book is available from the British
Library.

First edition: November 1997
1 3 5 7 9 10 8 6 4 2

Printed in Italy.

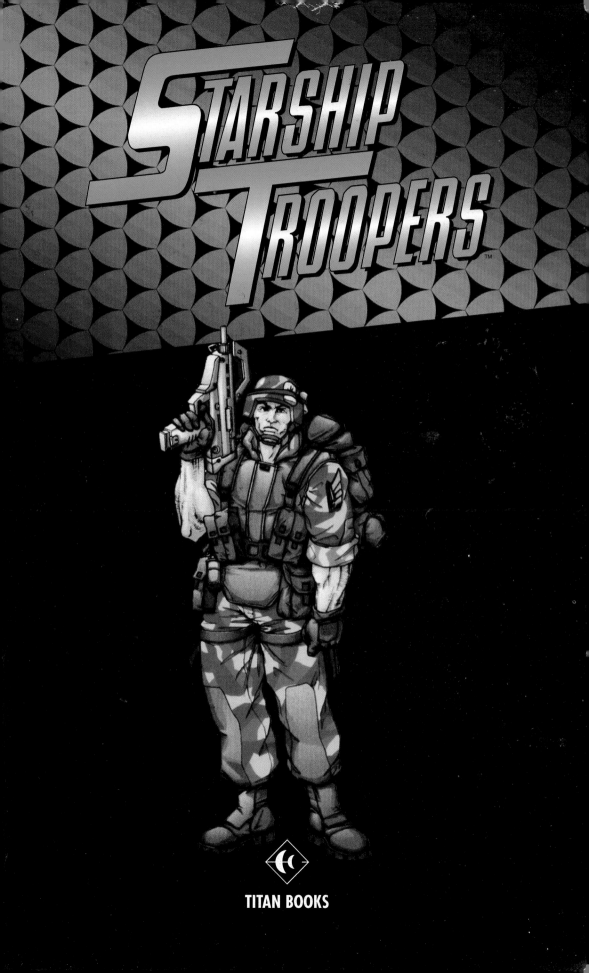

STARSHIP TROOPERS™

TITAN BOOKS

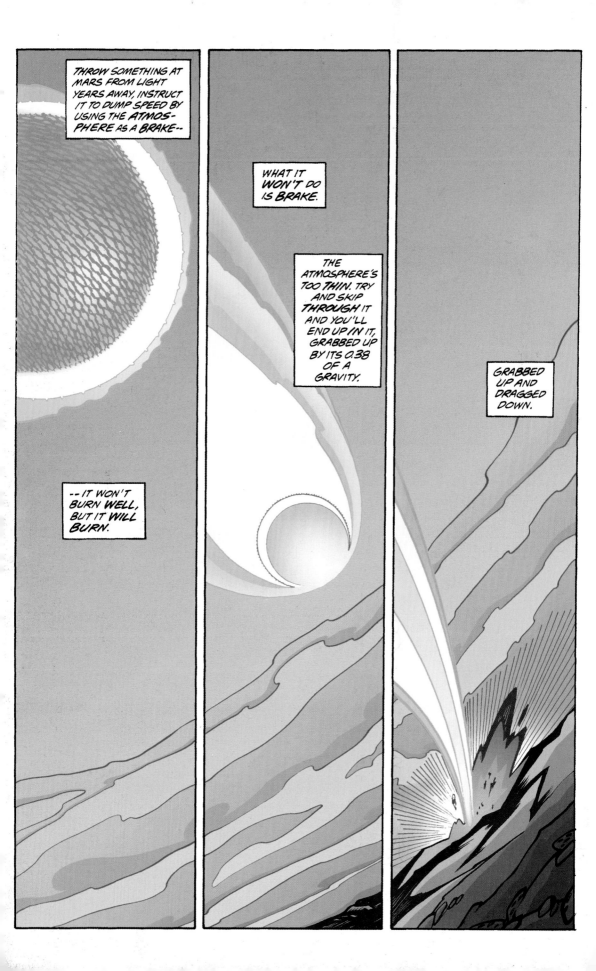

THROW SOMETHING AT MARS FROM LIGHT YEARS AWAY, INSTRUCT IT TO DUMP SPEED BY USING THE *ATMOSPHERE* AS A BRAKE--

-- IT WON'T BURN *WELL*, BUT IT *WILL* BURN.

WHAT IT *WON'T DO* IS *BRAKE*.

THE ATMOSPHERE'S TOO *THIN*. TRY AND SKIP *THROUGH* IT AND YOU'LL END UP *IN* IT, GRABBED UP BY ITS 0.38 OF A GRAVITY.

GRABBED UP AND DRAGGED DOWN.

AND INSECT JUICES CRACKLE ON FREEZING, HUMAN-OWNED SOIL, FULLY THIRTY YEARS BEFORE THE FIRST INTERSTELLAR WAR.

FEDERAL MILITARY
COMMUNICATIONS NET
ENCRYPTION LEVEL MAJESTIC

WAITING...

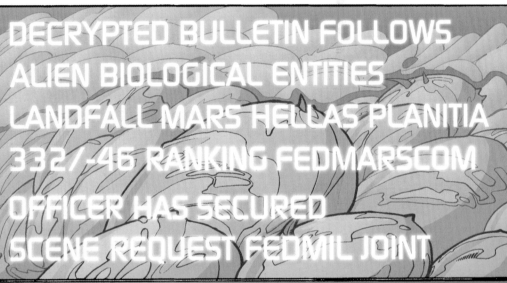

DECRYPTED BULLETIN FOLLOWS
ALIEN BIOLOGICAL ENTITIES
LANDFALL MARS HELLAS PLANITIA
332/-46 RANKING FEDMARSCOM
OFFICER HAS SECURED
SCENE REQUEST FEDMIL JOINT

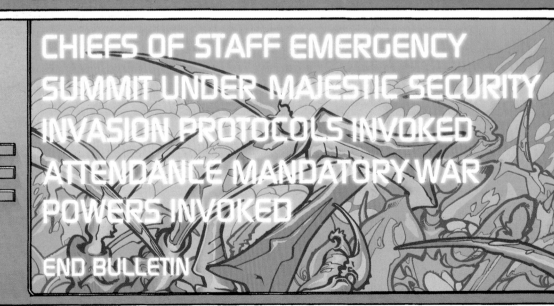

CHIEFS OF STAFF EMERGENCY
SUMMIT UNDER MAJESTIC SECURITY
INVASION PROTOCOLS INVOKED
ATTENDANCE MANDATORY WAR
POWERS INVOKED

END BULLETIN

ONE YEAR LATER.

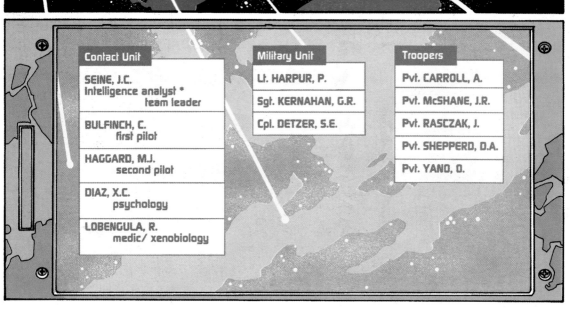

Contact Unit	Military Unit	Troopers
SEINE, J.C. Intelligence analyst * team leader	Lt. HARPUR, P.	Pvt. CARROLL, A.
BULFINCH, C. first pilot	Sgt. KERNAHAN, G.R.	Pvt. McSHANE, J.R.
HAGGARD, M.J. second pilot	Cpl. DETZER, S.E.	Pvt. RASCZAK, J.
DIAZ, X.C. psychology		Pvt. SHEPPERD, D.A.
LOBENGULA, R. medic/ xenobiology		Pvt. YANO, O.

BULFINCH?

BULFINCH, WAKE *UP.*

I WAS *RESTING* MY *EYES*, HAGGARD. I'VE *TOLD* YOU, I'M *NEVER* SLEEPING, JUST--

WE'RE READY TO CUT MAIN ENGINES. BRAKING AND ANTI-COLLISION SOLUTIONS ARE IN THE HELM MEMORY.

FIRST PILOT TO ALL POINTS--WE ARE *ENTERING* THE *KLENDATHU SYSTEM* AND ARE REDUC-ING FROM INTERSTELLAR SPEEDS AT TEN SECONDS FROM MY MARK...

...MR. *SEINE* TO THE *BRIDGE*, PLEASE...

...*MARK.*

DIAZ? COME *IN* HERE.

TIME FOR YOUR FIRST *PSYCHOLOGICAL PROFILE.*

THE ALIENS HAVE NO LONG-RANGE COMMUNICATION, *THEORIES?*

WHAT'S UP? DID HAGGARD FINALLY KILL BULFINCH? OR DID SHE ACTUALLY CRACK AND MAKE SOME TEA?

HM.

TWO POSSIBILITIES-- A CIVILIZATION *SO* STRICT AND INFLEXIBLE THAT COMMUNICATION, EXCEPT IN CLOSE RANGE, IS *DISALLOWED?*

SO, *WHAT?* THEY COLONIZE A WORLD AND NEVER SPEAK TO THEIR COLONISTS *AGAIN?*

I'M BRINGING UP THE *BUFFER* GENERATORS... DENSE SPACE AHEAD...

SECOND POSSIBILITY?

HEY, I SAID IT WAS JUST A *POSSIBILITY.* MAYBE THE CULTURE ONLY RECOGNIZES COMMUNICATION BETWEEN *EQUALS.*

THERE'S NOBODY *ON* KLENDATHU AND WE'VE COME A VERY LONG WAY FOR *NOTHING.*

HEY, YOU *ASKED.*

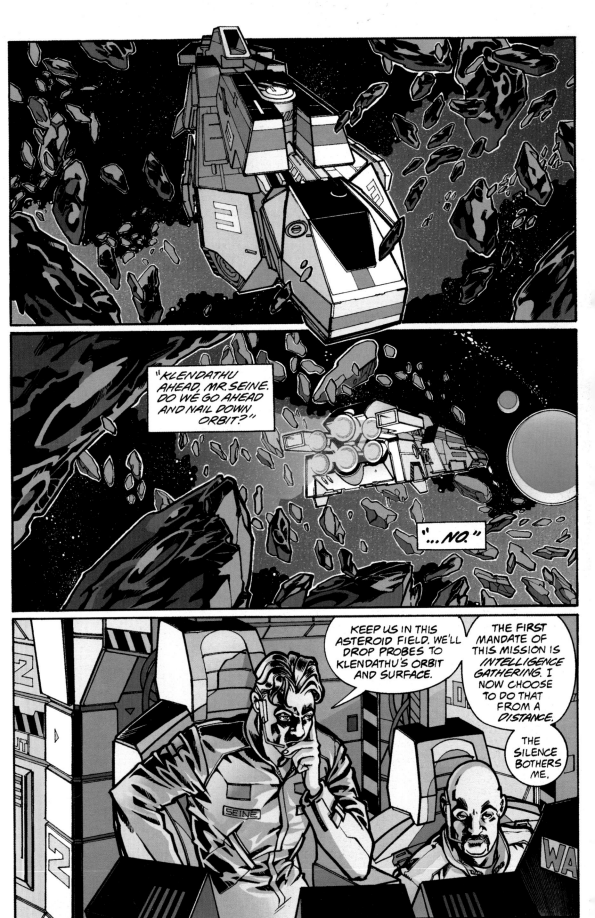

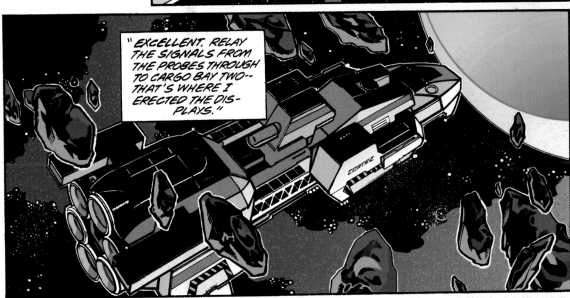

"EXCELLENT. RELAY THE SIGNALS FROM THE PROBES THROUGH TO CARGO BAY TWO-- THAT'S WHERE I ERECTED THE DISPLAYS."

MR. SEINE, QUESTION; ARE WE ABSOLUTELY POSITIVE THAT WE'RE IN THE RIGHT PLACE?

THE MARS ENTITY WAS DEFINITELY LAUNCHED FROM KLENDATHU, YES.

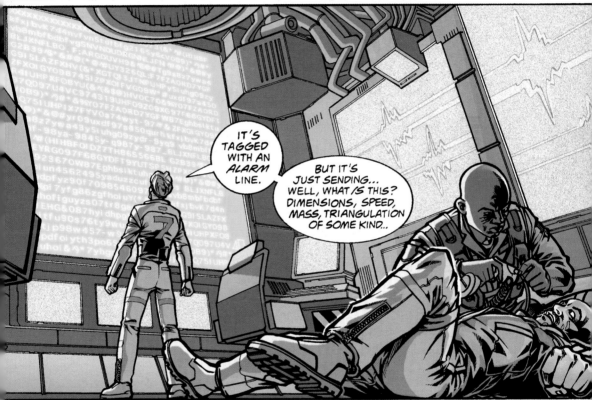

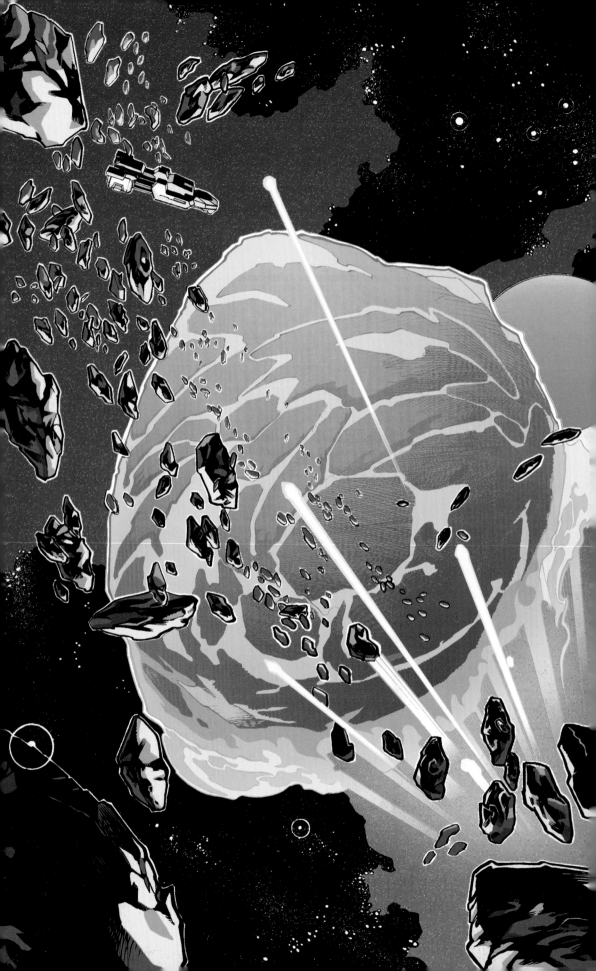

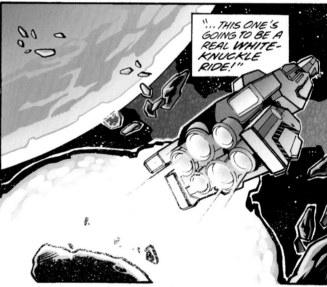

CLEAR... WE'RE CLEAR.

I DON'T BELIEVE IT, BUT WE'RE CLEAR.

STAND DOWN, HAGGARD.

DIAZ-- *DAMAGE REPORT!*

HULL INTEGRITY IS HOLDING. GOT A FEW MINOR BREACHES-- AFFECTED SECTIONS ARE SEALED OFF AND *AUTO-REPAIR SYSTEMS* ARE COMPENSATING.

MAIN DRIVE AND WEAPONS SYSTEMS ARE DOWN. AUTO-REPAIR IS RUNNING DIAGNOSTICS NOW.

COMMANDER SEINE...?

I KNOW...

...WE CAN'T GO ANYWHERE AND WE CAN'T SHOOT BACK AT ANYONE *SHOOTING* AT US.

UNTIL AUTO-REPAIR BRINGS THOSE SYSTEMS BACK ON-LINE, WE'RE A *SITTING TARGET* UP HERE IN ORBIT.

ONLY ONE CHOICE -- LAND ON KLENDATHU AND GO STRAIGHT INTO *FIRST CONTACT.*

HAGGARD, PREP THE *DROP SHUTTLE* FOR IMMEDIATE USE AND TELL OUR PASSENGERS IN BAY THREE THAT, AS OF NOW, THEY'RE NO LONGER JUST ALONG FOR THE RIDE...

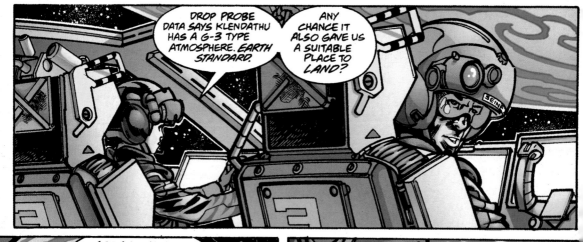

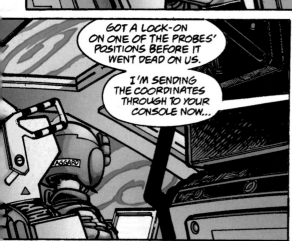

OKAY, WE'RE DOWN. YOUR PEOPLE READY FOR DEPLOYMENT, HARPUR?

WE'RE *MOBILE INFANTRY*, COMMANDER, WE WERE *BORN* READY.

JUST POINT US AT THEM AND GIVE US THE WORD.

UHHH... RIGHT. MISSION PARAMETERS SAY *YOU* HAVE TACTICAL COMMAND IN THE EVENT OF A HOSTILE FIRST-CONTACT SITUATION.

ALL RIGHT, PEOPLE, YOU HEARD THE MAN. THIS IS *OUR SHOW* NOW!

KERNAHAN AND *DETZER*-- TAKE YOUR SQUADS OUT AND SECURE THE *L.Z.* LET'S SHOW THE CIVILIANS HOW WE DO THINGS IN THE *M.I.!*

YEAH... TELL ME ABOUT IT...

OUR LIVES, IN THEIR HANDS.

NOW *THERE'S* A COMFORTING THOUGHT...

HEY, CARROLL, YOU EVER BEEN TO WYOMING?

NO. WHY?

BECAUSE THAT'S WHAT THIS PLACE REMINDS ME OF. WYOMING.

ONLY WITHOUT THE SAME *WILD NIGHTLIFE SCENE...*

SERGEANT KERNAHAN-- I GOT SOMETHING HERE!

LOOKS LIKE ONE OF THE *DROP PROBES* FROM THE *CORTEZ--!*

KERNAHAN TO HARPUR. WE'VE FOUND ONE OF THE DROP PROBES. IT'S DAMAGED AND BURIED IN SOME KIND OF *SINKHOLE* IN THE GROUND.

UNDER-STOOD, KERNAHAN...

...MUST HAVE *IMPACTED* ON LANDING. DIG IT OUT OF THERE AND BRING IT BACK TO THE SHUTTLE. MAYBE THE CIVILIANS CAN RETRIEVE SOME HARD DATA FROM ITS INSTRUMENTATION.

THE PROBES ARE DESIGNED FOR SOFT LANDING. WHAT'S IT DOING IN THE *GROUND?*

I DON'T LIKE THIS, HARPUR. FORGET THE PROBE AND PULL YOUR PEOPLE BACK TO THE SHUTTLE.

THIS IS AN M.I. OPERATION, COMMANDER. LIKE YOU SAID, I HAVE TACTICAL COMMAND HERE...

TIME-OUT, BOYS! ONBOARD GYROS ARE PICKING UP SOME KIND OF SEISMIC DISTURBANCE!

CAN'T GET A FIX ON IT... IT'S COMING FROM ALL AROUND US!

I'M INVOKING COMMAND AUTHORITY, HARPUR. THIS MISSION IS BACK UNDER MY CONTROL!

IT'S DUG IN DEEP. WHAT'S THE MATTER, McSHANE? AFRAID TO RUIN YOUR MANICURE?

GET DOWN HERE AND GIVE ME A HAND!

KERNAHAN, THIS IS SEINE. GET YOUR PEOPLE OUT OF THERE NOW! THAT'S AN ORDER!

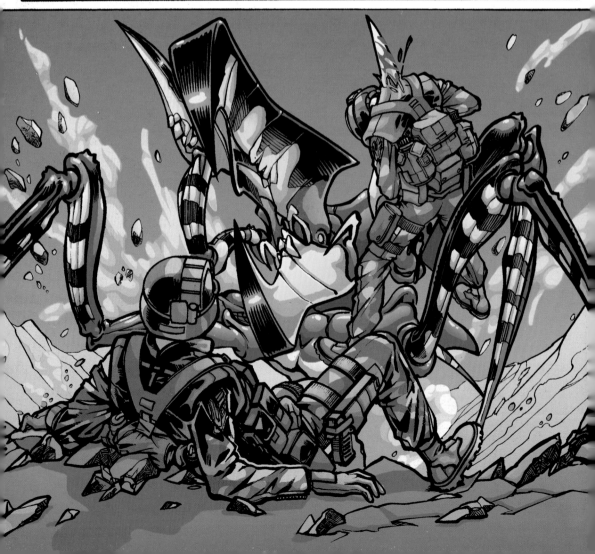

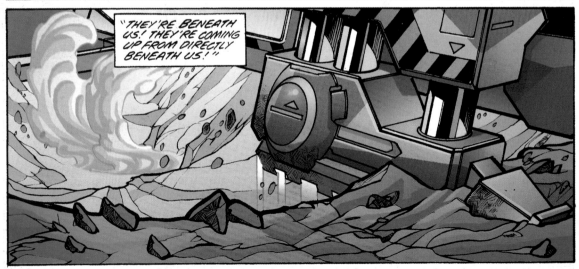

"REAR LANDING LEGS ARE GONE... OH, GOD, WE'RE GOING DOWN--!"

EVERYONE OKAY?

HAGGARD. SYSTEMS CHECK. *NOW.*

OH, GOD, IT'S *HARPUR*--

"--IT'S HARPUR. HE'S OUT THERE, AND HE'S STILL ALIVE!"

GG~GGG-- GHHK

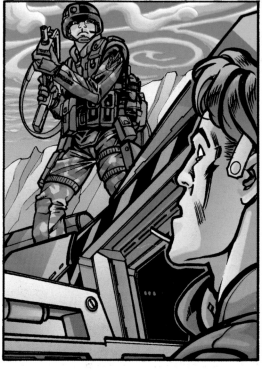

...AS A XENOBIOLOGIST, I CAN ONLY SAY THAT IT MAKES FOR MOST...UM...INTER-ESTING VIEWING.

THERE APPEAR TO BE SEVERAL *BREEDING SITES* LOCATED ON THE PLANET'S SURFACE.

THE CREATURES FOLLOW THE CLASSIC *HIVE-INSECT SPECIES* BEHAVIOR PATTERNS. WHEN THEY BREED, THEY BREED IN THE *THOUSANDS.*

THESE CREATURES APPEAR TO BE A *WARRIOR SUBCLASS* OF THE MAIN SPECIES. THEY *FIGHT* BEFORE THEY MATE, ENSUR-ING THAT ONLY *THE STRONGEST* SURVIVE TO BREED.

"*MATING AND EATING,*" JUST LIKE BULFINCH SAID--

I'M SURE THIS IS *FASCINATING* TO ANOTHER XENOBIOLOGIST, LOBENGULA...REAL CAREER-MAKING STUFF...

...BUT HOW EXACTLY IS IT RELEVANT TO *OUR* SITUATION?

TO BE CONCLUDED!

FEDMIL OPERATION 378/- 93
RECON CRUISER CORTEZ
SHIP'S LOG ENTRY UPDATE
TEAM XENOBIOLOGIST
LOBENGULA, R. REPORTING

MISSION OBJECTIVE: INITIATE
FIRST CONTACT WITH UNKNOWN
SPECIES, PLANET DESIGNATE
KLENDATHU

MISSION STATUS:
COMPROMISED

--NUMBER ONE-- WHILE THE CREATURES ARE STILL ENGAGED IN THEIR MATING RITUAL, IT MAY BE POSSIBLE FOR YOU TO LEAVE THE CRAFT AND CARRY OUT EXTERNAL REPAIRS ON THE PROPULSION SYSTEM.

HOWEVER, I SHOULD WARN YOU THAT YOUR PRESENCE OUT-SIDE THE CRAFT MAY TRIGGER OFF AN IMMEDIATE ATTACK RESPONSE.

UH-HUH. AND THE SECOND POSSIBILITY?

THE CORTEZ'S DRIVE SYSTEMS ARE BACK ON-LINE. FAILING YOUR RETURN FROM THE PLANETARY SURFACE, I BELIEVE I CAN SHOOT ENOUGH ANTI-PSYCHO-TICS INTO MR. BULFINCH TO ENABLE HIM TO PILOT THE SHIP HOME.

I'M SORRY, BUT FEDMIL COMMAND MUST BE MADE AWARE OF THE THREAT THESE CREATURES REPRESENT.

AS ACTING MISSION COMMANDER, MY REPORT WILL SHOW THAT YOU ALL FULFILLED YOUR DUTIES TO THE BEST OF YOUR ABILITIES.

UNDERSTOOD, LOBENGULA. IF IT MAKES ANY DIFFERENCE, I'D HAVE DONE THE SAME THING IN YOUR POSITION...

CORPORAL DETZER!

SIR?

WITH HARPUR AND KERNAHAN GONE, YOU'RE NEXT IN THE CHAIN OF COMMAND, DETZER...

ARE YOUR PEOPLE READY FOR DE-PLOY-MENT?

D-DEPLOYMENT, SIR? WITH WHAT...?

THERE'S ONLY THREE OF US LEFT, AND--

WE'RE READY. WHAT DO YOU WANT US TO DO?

WE'RE GOING BACK OUTSIDE, I NEED YOU TO BUY US SOME TIME WHILE WE BRING THE LIFTER SYSTEMS BACK ON-LINE.

DIAZ-- YOU'RE STAYING IN HERE. HAGGARD--

YOU WANT ME TO GO OUT THERE, DON'T YOU? I'M THE ONLY ONE QUALIFIED TO REPAIR THE LIFTERS.

YOU WANT ME TO GO OUT THERE, AND THOSE THINGS ARE GOING TO KILL ME...

NO THEY WON'T. BECAUSE I'LL BE OUT THERE WITH YOU, AND I WON'T LET THEM.

TRUST ME, HAGGARD. I WON'T LET THEM KILL ANY MORE OF MY PEOPLE.

MR. RASCZAK. AS TEAM LEADER ON THIS MISSION, I THOUGHT I WAS FAMILIAR WITH EVERY ITEM ON OUR CARGO MANIFEST.

WHAT EXACTLY ARE *THOSE*, AND WHERE DID THEY COME FROM?

NEXT-GEN M.I. WEAPONRY. PROTOTYPE M-85 *TAC-NUKE MISSILE LAUNCHER.*

THEY DON'T APPEAR ON THE MANIFEST BECAUSE THEY AREN'T SUPPOSED TO EXIST YET. LET'S JUST SAY WE BROUGHT THEM ALONG FOR *INSURANCE.*

YOU'RE *KIDDING*, RIGHT? YOU'RE NOT ACTUALLY GOING TO USE THOSE THINGS OUT THERE?

COMMANDER SEINE, YOU CAN'T SERIOUSLY SANCTION USING THOSE WEAPONS! WE DON'T KNOW ANY-THING ABOUT THEIR EFFECTS!

THEN WHAT DO YOU SUGGEST WE DO, LADY? HOSE DOWN THOSE THINGS WITH COLD WATER? BESIDES, THE WARHEAD PAYLOAD IS *LOW-YIELD.* MINIMAL RADIATION EFFECT.

WORST CASE SCENARIO, WE ALL GO HOME WITH DEEP SUNTANS.

AGREED.

EVERYONE READY? HAGGARD, STAND BY ME--

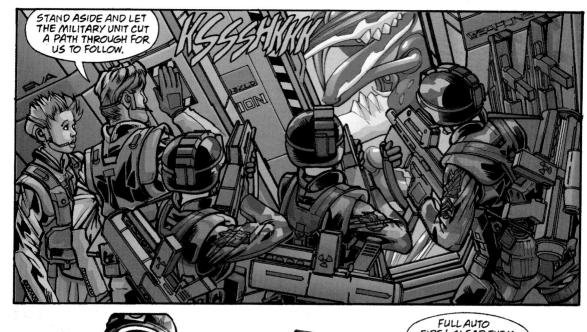

MR. SEINE, WHATEVER YOU'VE GOT TO DO, I SUGGEST YOU DO IT QUICKLY.

DETZER! THREE OF THEM, COMING OVER THE TOP OF THE HULL!

I SEE 'EM...

YOU AND CARROLL SECURE THE AREA AROUND THE SHUTTLE. I'LL COVER THE CIVILIANS!

LIKE THE MAN SAID, I SUGGEST WE MOVE ON, SIR. ME AND MR. MORITA HERE WILL BE WATCHING YOUR TAILS.

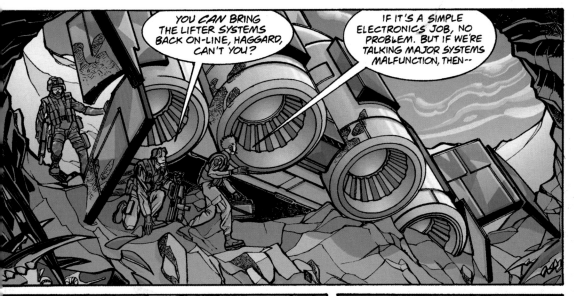

YOU *CAN* BRING THE LIFTER SYSTEMS BACK ON-LINE, HAGGARD, CAN'T YOU?

IF IT'S A SIMPLE ELECTRONICS JOB, NO PROBLEM. BUT IF WE'RE TALKING MAJOR SYSTEMS MALFUNCTION, THEN--

LOOK OUT!

DO IT, HAGGARD.

JUST DO IT, AND GET WHAT'S LEFT OF MY MISSION TEAM OUT OF HERE.

RASCZAK! RUN! THEY'RE RIGHT *BEHIND* YOU!

AAH!

CHLAK!

"HOW WILL THE SERPENT EVER LOSE ITS VENOM, WHILE THE SERVANTS OF GOD POSSESS THE SAME DISPOSITION, AND CONTINUE TO MAKE WAR UPON IT?

"MEN MUST BECOME HARMLESS BEFORE THE BRUTE CREATION, AND WHEN MEN LOSE THEIR VICIOUS DISPOSITIONS AND CEASE TO DESTROY THE ANIMAL RACE...

"...THE LION AND THE LAMB CAN DWELL TOGETHER."

--JOSEPH SMITH, FOUNDER OF THE CHURCH OF JESUS CHRIST OF LATTER-DAY SAINTS

1

"A BUG IS ONE TOUGH **S.O.B.** YOU CAN BURN OFF THREE LEGS AND IT JUST KEEPS COMING. ONCE IT GRABS HOLD OF YOU, IT DOESN'T **LET GO.**

"ITS JAWS SECRETE AN **ANTI-COAGULANT** THAT BURNS LIKE HELL AND KEEPS YOUR BLOOD FROM CLOTTING, HELPING YOU TO **BLEED** TO DEATH.

"IT HAS NO EGO, NO FEAR OF DEATH, NO **THOUGHT** BUT TO KILL AND KILL AND KILL FOR THE GOOD OF THE HIVE.

"IT DOES NOT NEGOTIATE. IT DOES NOT BARGAIN. IT KILLS. PERIOD. A **TROOPER'S** JOB IS TO KILL IT FIRST."

--JEAN RASCZAK, MOBILE INFANTRYMAN

2

ANY QUESTIONS?

MISTER MYERS.

MISTER RASCZAK, IT SOUNDS LIKE THE BUGS ARE, WELL... **MINDLESS.**

NOT AT ALL.

EACH BUG IS PART OF A **COLLECTIVE,** JUST AS YOU AND I ARE PART OF THE COLLECTIVE KNOWN AS THE **TERRAN FEDERATION.**

THE BUG'S **STRENGTH** COMES FROM ITS WILLINGNESS TO SACRIFICE ITSELF FOR THE COMMON GOOD. WHAT IS ITS PARALLEL IN OUR OWN SOCIETY?

MISS VELKES.

CITIZENS... THOSE PEOPLE WHO'VE COMPLETED THEIR FEDERAL SERVICE AND HAVE EARNED THE RIGHT TO **VOTE.**

EXACTLY RIGHT.

AND WHY DO NON-CITIZENS TOLERATE THIS ARRANGEMENT?

UHM, BECAUSE THEY REALIZE IT'S IN THEIR BEST INTEREST?

WRONG!

IT IS **FORCED** UPON THEM BY THE STRONGEST MEMBERS OF SOCIETY--THE **ONLY** MEMBERS TO PROVE THAT THEY PUT SOCIETY'S NEEDS ABOVE THEIR PERSONAL SURVIVAL!

ALL RIGHT, EVERYBODY **OUT!** GO FIND YOUR-SELVES CUSHY CIVILIAN JOBS...

BRRIING

...AND DON'T EVEN **THINK** ABOUT FEDERAL SERVICE.

HAVE A NICE **LIFE.**

THAT'S **ONE** CLASS I'M GLAD TO BE THROUGH WITH! RASCZAK'S A PRIME CANDIDATE FOR A **PADDED CELL.**

HE'S MORE OF A MAN THAN **YOU'LL** EVER BE.

HISTORY AND MORAL PHILOS JEAN R INSTR

WOW!

PEACEFUL COEXISTENCE "AND THE LION SHALL L WITH TH LAMB"

HOW DO THEY **DO** THAT?

IT'S EASY...

...NOW AND AGAIN, THEY THROW IN MORE LAMBS.

BEEP BEEP BEEP

POPCOR

YEAH.

RASCZAK, I'VE GOT AN ASSIGNMENT FOR YOU.

NOT INTERESTED. I'VE TAUGHT MY LAST CLASS, REMEMBER? NEXT WEEK I'M BACK ON ACTIVE DUTY.

CHANGE OF PLANS. YOU LEAVE THIS AFTERNOON FOR DANTANA.

DANTANA...THREE HUNDRED MORMON EXTREMISTS HAD JUST SETTLED THERE. THE PROBLEM WAS, THE DANTANA SYSTEM WAS INSIDE THE ARACHNID QUARANTINE ZONE...

...BUG TERRITORY.

SINCE THEY LOST UTAH IN THE UPRISINGS, THE MORMONS HAD BEEN ON THE RUN. JUST LIKE OLD TIMES.

DESPERATION HAD TAKEN THE MOST RADICAL GROUP TO DANTANA...THAT, AND STUBBORN-NESS.

TURNS OUT, THE COLONISTS HAD JUST CERTIFIED THEIR FIRST GRADUATING CLASS.

UNFORTUNATELY, THEY'D LEFT ONE COURSE OUT OF THE CURRICULUM, A COURSE THEY FOUND OBJECTION-ABLE AS A MATTER OF PRINCIPLE...

...MINE. HISTORY AND MORAL PHILOSOPHY.

H&MP WAS MANDATORY. A STUDENT DIDN'T HAVE TO PASS IT, BUT HE HAD TO SHOW UP AND STAY AWAKE WHILE A CITIZEN LIKE ME TRIED TO POUND SOMETHING LIKE A MORAL SENSE INTO HIS SKULL.

THE MORMONS FIGURED THAT WAS THEIR JOB, AND THAT THE TEACHINGS OF JOSEPH SMITH TOOK PRECEDENCE OVER THOSE OF THE TERRAN FEDERATION.

THE FEDERATION DIDN'T SEE IT THAT WAY.

5

NO COLLEGE IN THE FEDERATION WOULD **TOUCH** THE MORMON GRADS.

I WASN'T EXPECTING A WARM WELCOME.

MY NAME IS **EDWARD ALLEN**, CHIEF ADMINISTRATOR OF THE COLONY. YOU'RE MISTER RASCZAK, I PRESUME?

EVENTUALLY THE COLONISTS AGREED TO FLY IN AN H&MP INSTRUCTOR TO TEACH A **CRASH COURSE** THAT WOULD BRING THE GRADS INTO COMPLIANCE.

I WOULDN'T CARE IF YOU GOT NAKED AND WORSHIPPED A **VACUUM CLEANER**. I JUST DON'T LIKE BEING THIS FAR INSIDE **BUG COUNTRY**.

YEAH. AND FOR THE RECORD, I'M AS DELIGHTED TO **BE** HERE AS YOU ARE TO **HAVE** ME.

I'M SORRY YOU FIND OUR RELIGION SO **OFFENSIVE**, NOT THAT YOU'RE THE FIRST TO DO SO.

I ASSUME THE REST OF MY "LUGGAGE" WILL BE DELIVERED TO MY QUARTERS.

OF COURSE.

INCIDENTALLY, MY SON **KIRTLAND** WILL BE AMONG YOUR PUPILS. I'VE GIVEN HIM THE TASK OF **REPORTING** ON YOUR PROGRESS.

AT LEAST **SOMEBODY**'LL BE PAYING ATTENTION.

6

...BUT I DOUBT IT.

DESPITE MYSELF, I WAS BEGINNING TO **LIKE** THESE PEOPLE. I LIKE **ANYBODY** WHO GIVES A DAMN.

THAT NIGHT, I WAS SCHEDULED TO MEET WITH ANY **COLONISTS** WHO **CARED** ENOUGH TO BRAVE A SUBZERO WIND CHILL FACTOR TO HEAR THE FEDERATION'S SIDE OF THINGS.

I ESTIMATED THE ATTENDANCE AT **ONE HUNDRED PERCENT.** THERE MIGHT HAVE BEEN ONE OR TWO WOMEN WHO STAYED HOME WITH SICK BABIES...

I LAID IT OUT PLAIN AND SQUARE. THEY WERE DISOBEYING **ONE** FEDERATION DECREE BY SETTLING INSIDE THE QUARANTINE ZONE.

THEY COULD DISOBEY THEM **ALL** IF THEY FELT LIKE IT, BUT IF THEY WANTED THEIR KIDS TO GO TO FEDERATION **COLLEGES,** THEY HAD TO MEET EDUCATIONAL STANDARDS, AND THAT MEANT H&MP.

THEY DIDN'T INTERRUPT. THEY DIDN'T ASK ANY QUESTIONS.

WHEN MY SPEECH WAS OVER-- THIRTY SECONDS AFTER MY INTRODUCTION--THEY FILED OUT QUIETLY, NEVER SPEAKING A WORD. IT WAS A GESTURE AS ELOQUENT AS AN UPRAISED FINGER.

THEIR SILENCE TOLD ME THAT THEY WOULD **SUBMIT,** AND IT TOLD ME EXACTLY WHAT THEY THOUGHT...

...OF **ME** AND THE FEDERATION.

I BEGAN TO SENSE THE **STRENGTH** AND **DETERMINATION** THAT HAD CARRIED THEM TO THIS BALL OF ROCK. THEY'D MADE IT THIS FAR ON THE STRENGTH OF THEIR **BELIEFS.**

UNFORTUNATELY, THOSE BELIEFS MAY HAVE LED THEM TO A **FATAL** MISJUDGMENT.

THE NEXT MORNING I FACED MY PUPILS, ALL **FOUR** OF THEM.

I SHOULD'VE FIGURED--OUT OF THREE HUNDRED COLONISTS, THE GRADUATING CLASS COULDN'T AMOUNT TO MUCH.

FIRST, I WANT TO URGE ALL OF YOU TO **FLEE** THIS SLICE OF PARADISE AT YOUR EARLIEST OPPORTUNITY. IN CASE NOBODY'S TOLD YOU, YOU'RE LIVING INSIDE THE **BUG ZONE**.

THEY GAVE THE PLANET A TOTAL **SWEEP** BEFORE WE LANDED. THERE AREN'T ANY ARACHNIDS HERE.

I DECIDED TO LET THEM IN ON A SECRET. "NO **ADULTS**, MAYBE," I SAID...

"...BUT THE BUGS HAVE THIS LITTLE **TRICK**. THEIR EGGS LAY **DORMANT** FOR A LONG TIME.

"THEY DON'T HATCH UNTIL THEY'RE NEEDED, LIKE WHEN SOMEBODY ENCROACHES ON THEIR **SPACE**."

BULL. HOW COULD AN **EGG** KNOW WHEN TO HATCH?

HOW DOES A **SEED** KNOW THE SUN'S SHINING?

HOW DOES A MUSHROOM SPORE KNOW IT **RAINED** IN THE NIGHT?

ANALOGIES ASIDE, WE THINK BUG EGGS CAN SENSE **VIBRATION**. THOSE WIND GENERATORS OF YOURS ARE LIKE A COMBINATION **ALARM CLOCK** AND **BEACON** TO THE BUGS.

I THINK YOU'RE JUST SORE AT THE ARACHNIDS BECAUSE ONE OF THEM ATE YOUR **ARM**.

YOU TELL HIM, KIRT!

8

I LOST MORE THAN AN **ARM** IN THAT BATTLE, KID! I LOST **FRIENDS**... GOOD **TROOPERS** WHO DIED KEEPING THE WORLD SAFE FOR **CIVILIANS** LIKE YOU!

HEY-- I'M **SORRY** ABOUT THAT!

BUT YOU NEVER EVEN **TRIED** TO **REASON** WITH THEM, DID YOU? YOUR FIRST IMPULSE WAS **VIOLENCE**! YOU JUST **SHOT FIRST** AND NEVER ASKED QUESTIONS!

WHAT COULD I **SAY**? THE KID HAD NOT ONE CLUE IN THE WHOLE BLESSED **UNIVERSE** WHAT HE WAS TALKING ABOUT. HE'D NEVER FACED A **BUG**.

SUDDENLY I FELT VERY **TIRED**.

YOUR INSTRUCTOR TENDS TO BE **CRANKY** THIS EARLY IN THE MORNING.

FORGET IT.

KRKRKRKRK

THEN I HEARD IT. A SOUND LIKE **BACON FRYING**. I'D HEARD IT BEFORE...ON **KLENDATHU**, BUG CENTRAL.

MISTER RASCZAK... WHAT'S THE MATTER?

KRKRKRKRK

RKRKRKRKR

IT WAS THE SOUND BUGS MAKE WHEN THEY **TUNNEL**. IT'S LIKE THE HISS OF A COBRA-- BY THE TIME YOU **HEAR** IT, IT'S TOO DAMNED LATE...

MISTER RASCZAK...?

12

13

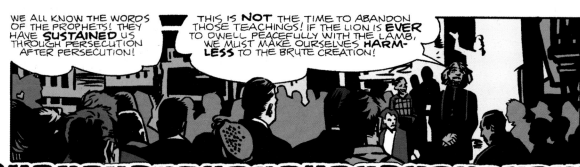

16

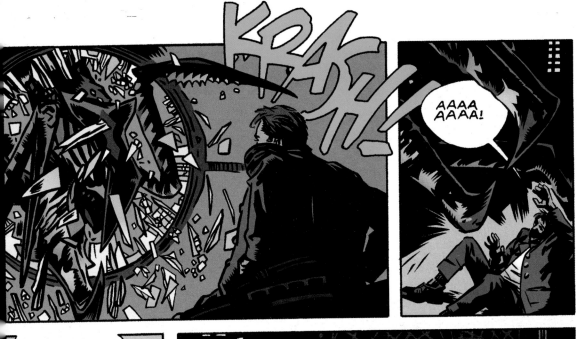

MAYBE THE KID USED THE RIGHT FREQUENCY TO HAIL THE SHIP... AND MAYBE NOT.

MAYBE THE RADIO OPERATOR WAS DILIGENTLY MONITORING THAT WAVELENGTH WHEN THE CALL CAME IN... AND MAYBE NOT.

MAYBE WE COULD STAY ALIVE FOR THE FIFTEEN MINUTES IT WOULD TAKE THE DROP SHIP TO REACH US...

...AND MAYBE NOT.

MONTHS LATER. PLANET P. WHISKEY OUTPOST.

WE ANSWERED A DISTRESS CALL. WHEN WE GOT HERE, THE PLACE LOOKED LIKE A **SLAUGHTER-HOUSE.**

THERE'RE MAYBE **FOUR** TROOPERS HERE I'D TRUST NOT TO CRACK UNDER THE PRESSURE OF A FULL-SCALE BUG ATTACK.

RICO. WATKINS. FLORES.

AND **KIRT ALLEN,** OF COURSE. HE GOT AS CLOSE TO THE DEMON AS ANYONE STILL ALIVE. BUT HE CLUNG TO HIS **SANITY,** SIGNED UP FOR FEDERAL SERVICE, AND EMERGED FROM BASIC TRAINING AS ONE DAMN FINE **TROOPER.**

THE OUT-POST IS A DEATH TRAP. WE'VE RADIOED FOR A DROP SHIP, BUT IT'S TAKING ITS SWEET TIME **GETTING** HERE.

NOTHING'S MOVING OUT THERE. EVERY-THING'S HUNKERED DOWN, **WAITING.** IT'S SO QUIET YOU CAN HEAR THE BLOOD **PULSE** IN YOUR BRAIN.

LORD, I **HATE** WHEN IT'S QUIET...

THE END

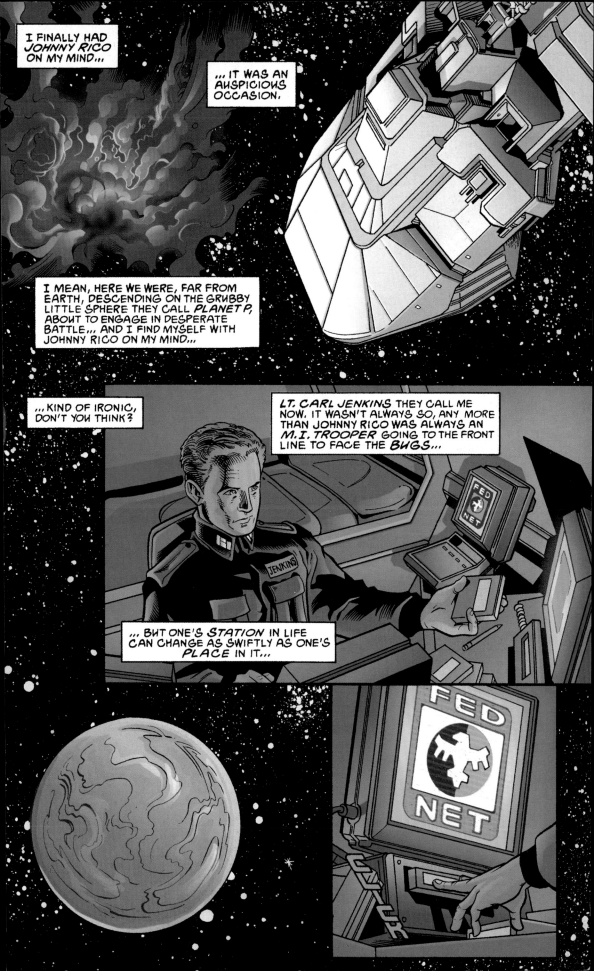

I FINALLY HAD *JOHNNY RICO* ON MY MIND...

...IT WAS AN *AUSPICIOUS OCCASION.*

I MEAN, HERE WE WERE, FAR FROM EARTH, DESCENDING ON THE GRUBBY LITTLE SPHERE THEY CALL *PLANET P,* ABOUT TO ENGAGE IN DESPERATE BATTLE... AND I FIND MYSELF WITH JOHNNY RICO ON MY MIND...

...KIND OF IRONIC, DON'T YOU THINK?

LT. CARL JENKINS THEY CALL ME NOW. IT WASN'T ALWAYS SO, ANY MORE THAN JOHNNY RICO WAS ALWAYS AN *M.I. TROOPER* GOING TO THE FRONT LINE TO FACE THE *BUGS...*

JENKINS

FED NET

...BUT ONE'S *STATION* IN LIFE CAN CHANGE AS SWIFTLY AS ONE'S *PLACE* IN IT...

FED NET

POOR JOHNNY...

YAGGHH!

SPLAT!

OH, GOD... PLEASE HELP ME...

RICO!

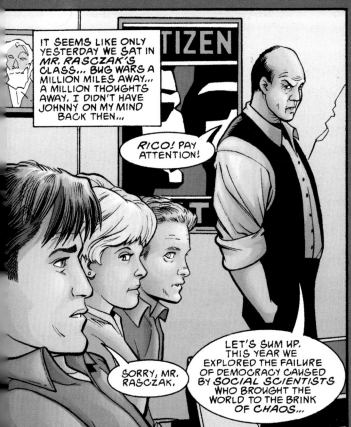

IT SEEMS LIKE ONLY YESTERDAY WE SAT IN MR. RASCZAK'S CLASS... BUG WARS A MILLION MILES AWAY... A MILLION THOUGHTS AWAY. I DIDN'T HAVE JOHNNY ON MY MIND BACK THEN...

RICO! PAY ATTENTION!

SORRY, MR. RASCZAK.

LET'S SUM UP. THIS YEAR WE EXPLORED THE FAILURE OF DEMOCRACY CAUSED BY SOCIAL SCIENTISTS WHO BROUGHT THE WORLD TO THE BRINK OF CHAOS...

... AND HOW THE VETERANS TOOK CONTROL AND IMPOSED A STABILITY THAT HAS LASTED GENERATIONS.

YOU. WHY ARE ONLY CITIZENS ALLOWED TO VOTE?

IT'S A REWARD, WHAT THE FEDERATION GIVES YOU FOR DOING FEDERAL SERVICE.

WRONG! WHEN YOU VOTE, YOU'RE EXERCISING POLITICAL AUTHORITY. YOU'RE USING FORCE!

FORCE IS VIOLENCE-- THE SUPREME AUTHORITY! POLITICAL AUTHOR- ITY IS VIOLENCE BY DECREE.

CITIZENS HAVE EARNED THE RIGHT TO USE IT.

HOW YOUNG WE WERE BACK THEN IN THAT BUENOS AIRES HIGH SCHOOL... HOW INEXPERIENCED, EVEN ME...

GEE, WE ALWAYS THOUGHT YOU WERE THE SUPREME AUTHORITY, MR. RASCZAK!

BRRIIING

VERY FUNNY, JENKINS.

THERE'S THE BELL. END OF ANOTHER SCHOOL YEAR. HAVE A NICE LIFE.

HEY! YOU WITH THE LEGS...

CARMEN IBANEZ. MAYBE I DIDN'T HAVE JOHNNY ON MY MIND BACK THEN, BUT HE CERTAINLY HAD CARMEN ON HIS... CONSTANTLY.

NOT HERE...

...C'MON, LET'S SEE IF THEY'VE POSTED THE MATH FINAL.

FIRST THING *FLEET ACADEMY* LOOKS AT IS YOUR MATH SCORES...

NINETY-SEVEN PERCENT! YES! NOW YOU, JOHNNY...

THIRTY-FIVE PERCENT. *OUCH.*

SORRY, JOHNNY.

HEY, MARCO! WAIT UP!

CAN'T STAND TO BE OUT OF YOUR SIGHT, THAT IT?

SHE'LL COME AROUND. I'M IN NO HURRY.

YEAH? WELL, LOOK AROUND. *OTHERS* ARE WAITING...

DIZZY LOVED JOHNNY, JOHNNY LOVED CARMEN, CARMEN COULDN'T MAKE UP HER MIND...

DIZZY FLORES? HOW DO YOU *KNOW?* READ HER MIND, CARL?

NO NEED FOR THAT. JUST LOOK AT HER.

DON'T FORGET ABOUT THIS AFTERNOON, RICO. YOU'RE ALWAYS LATE WHEN YOU WALK HER HOME TO FISH FOR A *KISS!*

GET OUT OF HERE, CARL!

HI, JOHNNY...

6

FROM THE *FEDERAL NET*-- ARE YOU *PSYCHIC?*

FED NET

IF YOU *THINK* YOU'RE PSYCHIC, MAYBE YOU ARE. *FEDERAL BENEFITS* ARE AVAILABLE FOR PSYCHIC CITIZENS. *WOULD YOU LIKE TO KNOW MORE?*

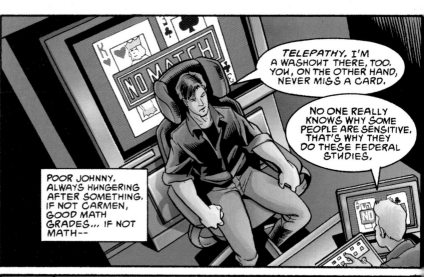

TELEPATHY. I'M A WASHOUT THERE, TOO. YOU, ON THE OTHER HAND, NEVER MISS A CARD.

NO ONE REALLY KNOWS WHY SOME PEOPLE ARE SENSITIVE. THAT'S WHY THEY DO THESE FEDERAL STUDIES.

POOR JOHNNY, ALWAYS HUNGERING AFTER SOMETHING. IF NOT CARMEN, GOOD MATH GRADES... IF NOT MATH--

YOU READING MY MIND RIGHT NOW, CARL?

DON'T GET PARANOID. I CAN'T DO HUMANS YET.

THINKING ABOUT SIGNING UP FOR FEDERAL SERVICE?

I THOUGHT YOU COULDN'T DO HUMANS.

BUT I WAS RIGHT. IF THINGS WERE TOUGH FOR JOHNNY AT SCHOOL, THEY WERE TWICE AS TOUGH AT HOME...

APPLYING FOR FEDERAL SERVICE? HAVE YOU LOST YOUR MIND? YOU'RE GOING TO HARVARD!

HEY, IT'S MY DECISION!

FEDERAL SERVICE IS REALLY JUST JOB TRAINING FOR INFERIOR PEOPLE SO THEY CAN CALL THEMSELVES "CITIZENS."

WAIT A MINUTE! CARL'S DOING HIS FEDERAL AND HE ISN'T INFERIOR! YOU'RE SAYING I'M NOT GOOD ENOUGH!

DID YOU HAVE TO DO THAT?

HE'LL CHANGE HIS MIND...

SLAM!

THAT WAS THE NIGHT OF THE BIG FAREWELL DANCE AT THE CENTER...

...AND ANY TIME JOHNNY COULD BE FOUND MOMENTARILY ALONE, WELL... DIZZY FLORES WAS ALWAYS RIGHT THERE.

HEY, RICO, WANNA DANCE?

HOW COME WE NEVER GOT TOGETHER, JOHNNY?

CAN'T WE JUST BE FRIENDS, DIZ?

"FRIENDS." THE FATAL WORD.

THERE'S MR. RASCZAK, LOOK, DIZ--

YOU'RE EXCUSED. GO, BEFORE I MAKE MYSELF LOOK EVEN STUPIDER.

--AND I WANT TO JOIN UP, MR. RASCZAK, I THINK I HAVE WHAT IT TAKES TO BE A CITIZEN, ONLY... MY FOLKS...

FIGURING THINGS OUT FOR YOURSELF IS THE ONLY FREEDOM ANYONE REALLY HAS. MAKE UP YOUR OWN MIND, RICO. THAT'S ALL I CAN OFFER.

JOHNNY! I WANT YOU TO MEET ZANDER! HE'S GOING TO BE A PILOT, TOO!

HELLO, ZANDER. GOOD-BYE, ZANDER, C'MON, CARMEN, IT'S THE LAST DANCE...

AND THE NEXT DAY...

...OF MY OWN FREE WILL, DO NOW ENROLL IN THE FEDERAL SERVICE OF THE TERRAN FEDERATION FOR NOT LESS THAN TWO YEARS AND AS MUCH LONGER AS MAY BE REQUIRED BY THE NEEDS OF THE SERVICE...

FRESH MEAT FOR THE GRINDER, HUH? HOW'D YOU KIDS DO?

I'M GOING TO BE A PILOT!

DID YOU GET STARSIDE R & D?

NO, GAMES AND THEORY.

WOW! GAMES AND THEORY! THAT'S MILITARY INTELLIGENCE!

NEXT TIME WE MEET, I'LL PROBABLY HAVE TO SALUTE YOU.

WHAT ABOUT YOU, SON?

INFANTRY, SIR!

WELL, GOOD FOR YOU!

THE MOBILE INFANTRY MADE ME THE MAN I AM TODAY!

AND SO WE WERE OFF. I WAS ASSIGNED TO CLASSIFIED TERRITORY, CARMEN TO THE *LUNA TERESHKOVA FLEET ACADEMY.* AND JOHNNY... WELL, IT WOULD BE SOME TIME BEFORE JOHNNY WAS ON MY MIND...

WELCOME TO CAMP CURRIE. I AM YOUR DRILL INSTRUCTOR, *SERGEANT ZIM!*

THE FIRST AND LAST WORDS OUT OF YOUR STINKING HOLE WILL BE "SIR." *GET ME?!*

SIR, YES, SIR!

AROUND THE ARMORY, MAGGOT! GO! GO! GO!

SIR, YES, SIR! OWW!

ANY TIME YOU WIMPS THINK I'M BEING TOO TOUGH YOU CAN SIGN THE 1240/A FORM AND TAKE A STROLL DOWN *"WASHOUT LANE"!*

YOU'RE LATE, SOLDIER!

SIR, RECRUIT FLORES REPORTING FOR DUTY, SIR!

YOU SPECIFICALLY REQUESTED TRANSFER TO THIS GROUP BECAUSE YOU HEARD IT WAS THE BEST. HMMM...

YEAH, WELL IT *IS* THE BEST, GRUNT. QUESTION IS, ARE *YOU* GOOD ENOUGH? LET'S SEE WHAT YOU *GOT!*

FOR BRIEF MOMENTS MY MIND DRIFTED TO JOHNNY. INFANTRY TRAINING WAS GRUELING. MY HEART WENT OUT TO HIM...

NICE THROW, RICO, YOU MIGHT ACTUALLY CRAWL UP TO SOLDIER LEVEL SOME DAY.

I DON'T UNDERSTAND...

CHIK!

...WHO NEEDS A KNIFE IN A *NUKE FIGHT*? WHAT'S THE POINT?!

PUT YOUR HAND ON THAT POST, TROOPER LEVY.

AGHH!

THE ENEMY CANNOT PUSH A BUTTON IF YOU DISABLE HIS HAND.

WHUK!

MEDIC!

WE HAVE ONE THING IN COMMON-- WE WERE ALL *STUPID* ENOUGH TO SIGN UP FOR MOBILE INFANTRY.

WHAT'S *YOUR* EXCUSE, DJANA'D?

POLITICS, YOU GOTTA BE A CITIZEN FOR THAT, SO HERE I AM. ACE?

ME, I'M GOING *CAREER*, OFFICER'S TRAINING.

WHAT ABOUT YOU, RICO?

HE'S HERE BECAUSE OF A GIRL...

WHILE MILES AWAY AND HIGH ABOVE, CARMEN WAS HAVING HER OWN KIND OF TRAINING...

-- BOOT CAMP'S TOUGH, BUT THEN I THINK OF YOU AND IT'S ALL WORTH IT. I MISS YOU. WRITE ME.

ORBIT IN FIVE, IBANEZ! FIRST ONE THERE GETS TO FLY!

LOCKING IT DOWN, SLOWPOKES!

OH, NO, NOT IBANEZ! SHE'S CRAZY!

WHOOMM

HOW COME YOU'RE IN SUCH A GOOD MOOD?

'CAUSE TODAY I GET TO FLY THAT!

LATER THAT DAY, CARMEN GOT HER BIG CHANCE ABOARD THE MAMMOTH STARSHIP, *RODGER YOUNG.*

TAKE THE NUMBER TWO CHAIR, IBANEZ. FOLLOW ALL INSTRUCTIONS OF YOUR SUPERVISOR.

ZANDER! YOU'RE MY *INSTRUCTOR?*

I HEARD ABOUT THIS CRAZY GIRL COMING THROUGH THE ACADEMY. WHEN IT TURNED OUT TO BE *YOU,* I MADE *SURE* WE'D RUN INTO EACH OTHER.

SHREEEEE

NICELY DONE, BUT NEXT TIME, DON'T EXCEED PORT SPEED.

PREPARE FOR *WARP.* DESIGN FOR JUPITER ORBIT.

YES, MA'AM, STAR DRIVE IN FIVE... FOUR... READY... STEADY...

VIIIPPPPPPP

...GO!

THAT DAY JOHNNY MADE SQUAD LEADER, BUT HE'D ONLY HAD HIS NEW CHEVRONS FOR A FEW HOURS WHEN THE BRIGHT DAY TURNED TO GLOOMY NIGHT...

OKAY, *MAIL CALL*. LEVY... SHUJUMI... RICO...

HI, JOHNNY...

... I'D HAVE WRITTEN SOONER, BUT... THEY'VE REALLY GOT US GOING HERE. THEY MUST HAVE MADE YOU SQUAD LEADER BY NOW, IF I KNOW YOU.

"I LOVE IT HERE, AND THAT'S ALSO THE *PROBLEM*. I THINK I'M GOING TO GO CAREER. I WANT A SHIP OF MY OWN, JOHNNY, AND THAT'S NOT GOING TO LEAVE A LOT OF TIME FOR *US*."

I KNOW THAT'S NOT WHAT YOU WANTED. BUT I HAVE TO FOLLOW MY HEART.

WRITE ME, OKAY? SO I'LL KNOW WE'LL ALWAYS BE *FRIENDS*.

FUNNY HOW THEY ALWAYS WANT TO BE *FRIENDS* AFTER THEY *RIP* YOUR GUTS OUT.

FROM THE FEDERAL NET --INSECT TRAGEDY ON DANTANA!

IGNORING FEDERAL WARNINGS, MORMON SETTLERS ESTABLISHED PORT JOE SMITH ON DANTANA, A SYSTEM JUST INSIDE THE *ARACHNID QUARANTINE ZONE*.

SEE THE BLOODY AFTERMATH TONIGHT AT SIX, ALL NET, ALL CHANNELS! *WOULD YOU LIKE TO KNOW MORE?*

WITH TRAINING IN HIGH GEAR, THERE WASN'T MUCH TIME FOR JOHNNY RICO TO INDULGE IN SELF-PITY...

NO MORE *FUN AND GAMES!* TODAY YOU USE *LIVE AMMO* IN A SIMULATED COMBAT ENVIRONMENT. IF YOU DO NOT GET YOUR TARGET, YOUR TARGET WILL GET *YOU!*

BRECKINRIDGE, RIGHT FLANK! DJANA'O, BRING UP THE REAR! MOVE OUT!

BRAAP BRAAP

UNGH!

HEY, MY *HELMET DISPLAY'S* FRITZED!

CRIPES, WHAT *NOW?* GIVE IT *HERE!*

HOW COME WHEN SOMETHING GOES WRONG, IT'S ALWAYS *YOU,* BRECKINRIDGE?

AW, SCREW YOU, D'JANAD...

I SWEAR-- *OOF!*

--!RRKKK!

WHAM!

BRECKINRIDGE!

OH, GOD, OH, GOD! I *TRIPPED!* IT WAS AN *ACCIDENT!*

ONE!

SNAP!

FOR *INCOMPETENCE OF COMMAND* AND *NEGLIGENCE* CONTRIBUTING TO THE *DEATH* OF A TEAMMATE, RECRUIT JOHN RICO IS SENTENCED TO *ADMINISTRATIVE PUNISHMENT*.

PROCEED, CORPORAL.

SO JOHNNY TOOK HIS LICKS, BUT STAYED ON, WHILE DJANA'D TOOK THE ENDLESS WALK DOWN WASHOUT LANE...

...AND A MILLION THOUGHTS AWAY, ONBOARD THE *RODGER YOUNG*...

COFFEE! THANKS, ZANDER, THIRD WATCH ALWAYS SEEMS TO LAST FOREVER.

DEPENDS ON WHO YOU'RE *SPENDING* IT WITH.

YOU KNOW, CAPTAIN DELADIER THINKS WE MAKE A GOOD TEAM. I CONCUR--

HOLD IT! MY GOD, ZANDER-- LOOK!

ASTEROID! CHRIST, IT'S HUGE! FIRE ENGINES!

STEADY... STEADY...

AND SO IT BEGAN, *WAR!* BETWEEN THE HUMANS AND THE ARACHNIDS.

TRAINING WAS OVER. THIS WAS THE REAL THING. THE FLEET SHIPS SURROUNDED THE UGLY LITTLE PLANET OF *KLENDATHU*...

LISTEN UP! WE'RE GOING IN WITH THE FIRST WAVE. THAT MEANS MORE *BUGS* FOR US TO KILL!. REMEMBER YOUR TRAINING AND YOU'LL MAKE IT BACK *ALIVE!*

WHILE JOHNNY DROPPED DOWN TO FIGHT, CARMEN MANNED THE *RODGER YOUNG* ABOVE HIM.

THE DROP SHIPS STREAMED TOWARD KLENDATHU.

BUG PLASMA, FROM THE PLANET! THIS ISN'T *RANDOM FIRE!* SOMEONE MADE A MISTAKE! WE'RE BEING *BOMBARDED!*

THERE GOES THE *GEORGE MARSHALL!*

SERGEANT, TAKE TWO SQUADS AND MOVE TO ASSAULT POINT ALPHA! WE HAVE TO TAKE OUT THOSE *BUG BATTERIES!*

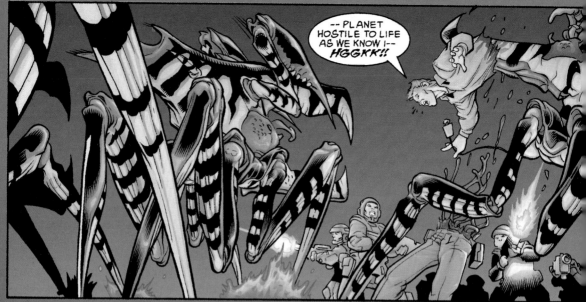

BR AAA

POOR JOHNNY.

YEAH, THAT WAS THE INVASION OF *KLENDATHU*, THE BUGS' HOME WORLD.

FTTZZ

THEY WERE A LOT SMARTER THAN I FIGURED, THE BUGS.

ME, LT. COLONEL CARL JENKINS, SUPPOSEDLY THE GUY WITH THE BIG *BRAINS.*

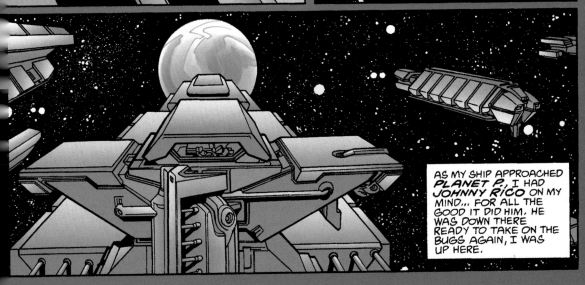

AS MY SHIP APPROACHED *PLANET P.,* I HAD *JOHNNY RICO* ON MY MIND... FOR ALL THE GOOD IT DID HIM. HE WAS DOWN THERE READY TO TAKE ON THE BUGS AGAIN, I WAS UP HERE.

JOHNNY'S OLD FLAME *CARMEN* AND HIS RIVAL *ZANDER* HAD BEEN ABOARD THE RODGER YOUNG DURING THE INVASION OF KLENDATHU.

THE STARSHIP DOCKED AT BATTLE STATION *TICONDEROGA* FOR REPAIRS.

YOU KNOW, FLEET ENCOURAGES MARRIAGE AMONG FLIGHT OFFICERS. I WAS THINKING...

UH, CARMEN...?

GOOD GOD, ZANDER, LOOK AT THE CASUALTIES...

BUGS DON'T TAKE PRISONERS.

OH, *NO*...

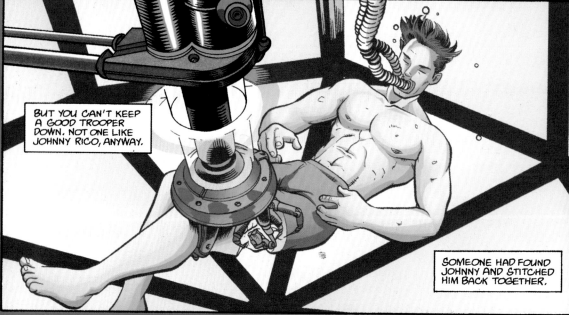

BUT YOU CAN'T KEEP A GOOD TROOPER DOWN. NOT ONE LIKE JOHNNY RICO, ANYWAY.

SOMEONE HAD FOUND JOHNNY AND STITCHED HIM BACK TOGETHER.

IN LESS THAN A WEEK JOHNNY AND HIS OLD PALS DIZZY AND ACE WERE BACK AT IT, WITH A NEW MOBILE INFANTRY COMPANY, THE *ROUGHNECKS*.

I HEAR THIS LIEUTENANT IS A REAL NUTBUSTER, DIZ.

ATTEN-SHUN!

JOHNNY, IT'S *MR. RASCZAK!* FROM SCHOOL!

THERE'S A NEW PLAN.

WE'RE GONNA CLEAN OUT THE SYSTEMS OUTLYING KLENDATHU ONE PLANET AT A TIME. GOT THAT, *ROUGH-NECKS?!*

RASCZAK'S ROUGHNECKS! YEAAHHHH!

IT'S A SMALL GALAXY, WITH ROOM FOR ONLY ONE AGGRESSIVE INTELLIGENCE.

SKWEEE

AFTER FLEET GLASSED TANGO URILLA...

VOOM!

... THE ROUGHNECKS MOPPED UP.

SPREAD OUT. WHEN YOU LOCATE A BUG HOLE, NUKE IT!

THERE'S THE HOLE! C'MON, SUGAR, LET'S BLOW IT!

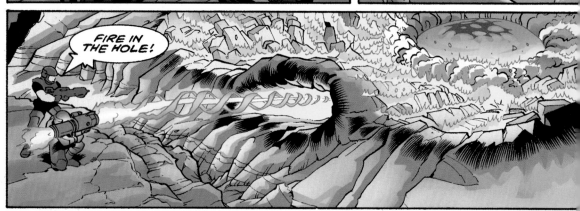

FIRE IN THE HOLE!

LOOKS LIKE WE WOKE 'EM UP!

HEADS UP! TANKER BUG!

HEADQUARTERS GOT A *DISTRESS CALL* FROM *PLANET P.* BY MORNING LIGHT THE ROUGHNECKS WERE THERE...

I'M GETTING *NOTHING* FROM THE OUTPOST. I'M GOING FOR HIGHER GROUND.

ROUGH-NECK PATROL TO WHISKEY OUTPOST... COME IN, WHISK--

--EEYAGGHH!

SUGAR... GIMME YOUR WEAPON.

BRAP

AK--

I EXPECT ANYONE HERE TO DO THE *SAME* FOR *ME.*

RICO, YOU'RE ACTING SERGEANT, *MOVE OUT!*

YOU HEARD THE LIEUTENANT, *SADDLE UP!*

SOMETHING HAD GONE **WRONG** AT WHISKEY OUTPOST. THE RAMP WAS DOWN, THE MAIN DOORS WERE CREAKING IN THE WIND...

JEEZ, SOMEBODY REALLY HUMPED THE BUNK...

THIS PLACE **CRAWLS.** I WANT IT SEALED TIGHT! LET'S GET OVER TO THE COMMUNICATIONS TENT.

GET ME AN UPLINK.

UH, LIEUTENANT--

FAR LEY

THEY SUCKED HIS **BRAINS** OUT!

THEY GET IN YOUR... **MIND**... THEY MAKE YOU... **DO THINGS!**

THEY MADE FARLEY CALL HEADQUARTERS...

GENERAL **OWEN!** SIR...?!

SO THE DISTRESS CALL WAS A **TRAP!**

RODGER YOUNG TO ROUGHNECK PATROL. WE HAVE PLANET P. AS CLEAR! WHAT'S GOING ON DOWN THERE?!

THIS PLACE *CRAWLS*, SIR! WE NEED PICKUP *NOW!*

SUGGEST YOU COME DOWN ON THIS TRANSMISSION! LANDING ZONE IS *EXTREMELY HOSTILE!*

INSIDE THE OUTPOST! THAT'S *CRAZY!*

HOPE YOU HAVE A CRAZY *PILOT!* OUT!

WATKINS, LEVY-- REINFORCE RIGHT!

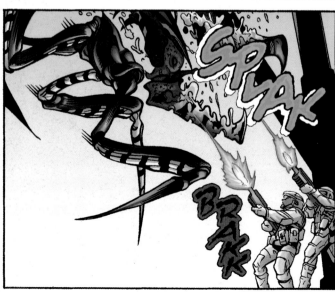

SPLAK

BLAK

LIEUTENANT! BOAT COMING DOWN, SIR!

FALL BACK INTO THE COMPOUND!

HEADS *UP!* TANKER!

HANG ON, DIZ! DON'T DIE ON ME!

JOHNNY... I'M... DYING...

NO, YOU'RE GONNA BE ALL RIGHT...

IT'S ALL RIGHT... 'CAUSE I GOT TO... HAVE YOU.

JOHNNY!

I..., WE THOUGHT YOU WERE DEAD!

NO, JUST MOST OF MY TROOPERS.

WOULD YA' GET ON THE COM AND TELL FLEET TO *GLASS* THAT ROCK?

NEGATIVE, THE SKY MARSHALL HAS OTHER PLANS FOR PLANET P.

"GREAT. M.I. DOES THE DYING, AND YOU GUYS JUST DO THE *FLYING*..."

THE DIFFERENCE BETWEEN A CITIZEN AND A CIVILIAN IS, A *CITIZEN* HAS THE *GUTS* TO MAKE THE SAFETY OF THE HUMAN RACE HIS RESPONSIBILITY.

DIZZY WAS A CITIZEN OF THE FEDERATION.

THAT BROUGHT US FULL CIRCLE. THAT BROUGHT JOHNNY AND ME TOGETHER AGAIN.

OFFICER ON DECK!

AT EASE, PEOPLE.

JOHNNY, I'M SORRY IT HAD TO BE YOUR UNIT ON PLANET P...

BUGS LAID A *TRAP*, DIDN'T THEY, CARL?

ELEGANT PROOF OF INTELLIGENCE, ISN'T IT? WE *THOUGHT* THERE MIGHT BE A *BRAIN* ON P.

YOU *KNEW* AND YOU SENT THEM ANYWAY?

WE COULDN'T AFFORD TO LAUNCH A FULL-SCALE OPERATION UNLESS WE WERE *SURE*.

HOPE YOU'RE READY FOR MORE, JOHNNY. WE'RE GOING BACK TO P TO *CAPTURE* THAT BRAIN.

THE *ROUGHNECKS* ARE *ALWAYS* READY, SIR.

I HEAR THE ROUGHNECKS NEED A NEW LIEUTENANT. WANT THE JOB?

AMONG THE TROOPS DEPLOYED FOR THE ASSAULT ON PLANET P...

ONE RULE. EVERYONE FIGHTS, NO ONE QUITS. DON'T DO YOUR JOB AND I'LL KILL YOU *MYSELF!*

RICO'S ROUGH-NECKS! WE'RE THE OLD MEN NOW, ACE.

THEY WERE LOOKING FOR A BUG NO ONE HAD EVER SEEN BEFORE... A *SMART* BUG... A *BRAIN* BUG... AND IT *KNEW* THEY WERE COMING...

HEAVY PLASMA OUT THERE! *EVASIVE ACTION!*

INITIATING STAR DRIVE IN--

"WE'RE *HIT!* WE'RE GOING DOWN! *ABANDON SHIP!*"

THE *RODGER YOUNG* JUST BURNED UP! IT'S ON THE RESCUE NET...

SURVIVORS?

DOESN'T LOOK GOOD, LIEUTENANT...

AT LEAST TWO CREW MEMBERS MANAGED TO GET TO A LIFE POD-- CARMEN AND ZANDER.

CONTROL'S SLUGGISH! WE'RE HEADED IN!

"LIFE POD ROMEO YANKEE SIX THREE, IS ANYONE RECEIVING? ROMEO YANKEE SIX THREE GOING IN!"

WHAM!

THIS IS ROUGHNECK PATROL. CARMEN, IS THAT YOU?

JOHNNY, IT'S ME! WE'RE TEN METERS SUBTERRA IN BUG CITY AT MAP POSITION GOLD FIVE! SITUATION IS--

BRAP

--EMINENTLY HOSTILE!

THREE CLICKS SOUTH BY SOUTHWEST... THERE!

I NEED VOLUNTEERS TO HELP PULL THEM OUT!

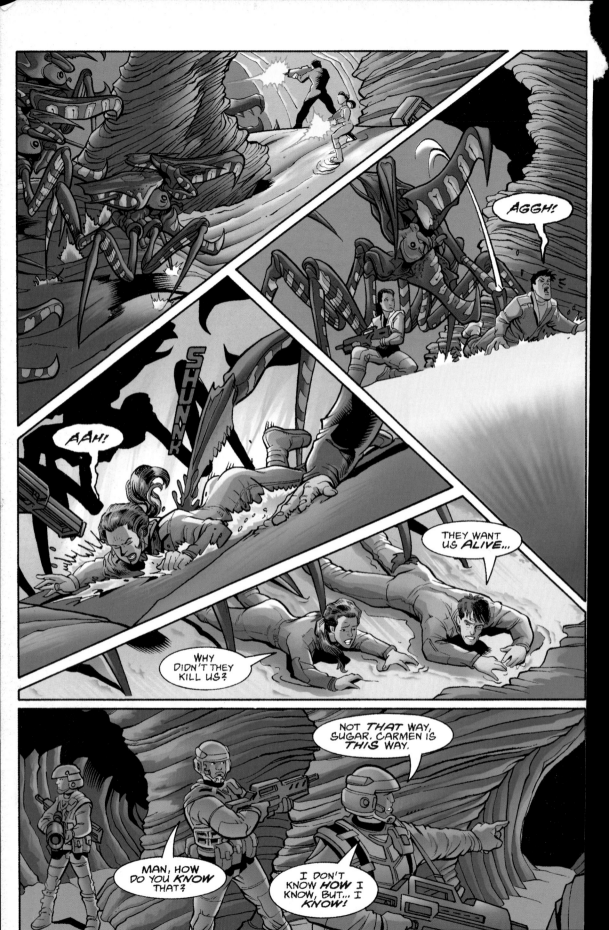

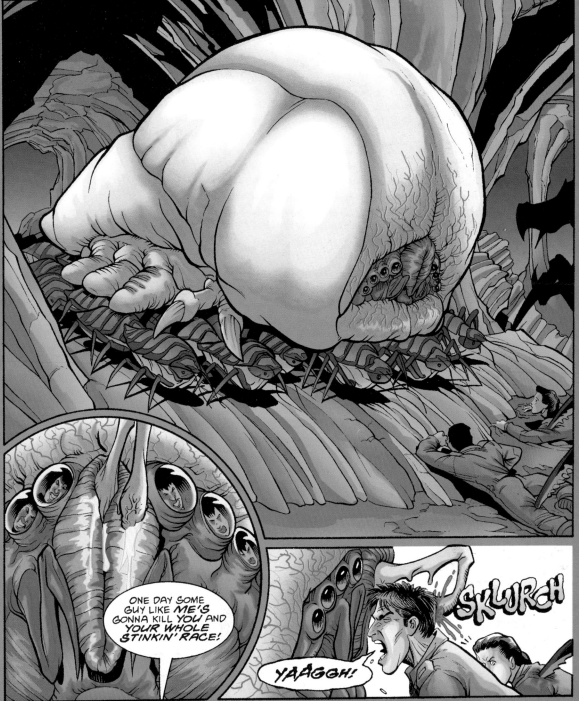

HEY, YOU WITH THE *EYES!* YOU KNOW WHAT *THIS* IS?!

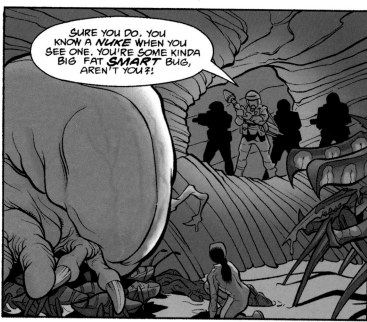

SURE YOU DO. YOU KNOW A *NUKE* WHEN YOU SEE ONE. YOU'RE SOME KINDA BIG FAT *SMART* BUG, AREN'T YOU?!

IT'S *ESCAPING!*

ROUGHNECK PATROL TO "A" COMPANY! BRAIN BUG EYEBALLED MOVING WEST OF MAP POSITION GOLF FIVE!

YAAH!

GIMME THE *NUKE!* I'M GONNA KILL ME SOME *BUGS!*

GO GO GO GO!

WHOOOMM!

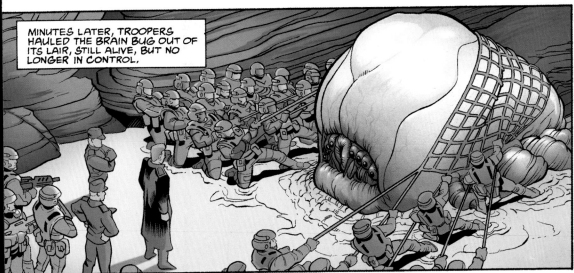

MINUTES LATER, TROOPERS HAULED THE BRAIN BUG OUT OF ITS LAIR, STILL ALIVE, BUT NO LONGER IN CONTROL.

WHAT'S IT THINKING, COLONEL?

IT'S AFRAID...

IT WAS YOU, WASN'T IT, CARL? *YOU* TOLD ME HOW TO FIND CARMEN. I THOUGHT YOU COULDN'T *DO* HUMANS...

WELL, THAT'S CLASSIFIED.

WE'VE GOT ONE OF THEIR *BRAINS* NOW. PRETTY SOON WE WILL KNOW HOW THEY *THINK*, HOW TO *BEAT* THEM.

"Insect Touch"

Warren Ellis & Gordon Rennie — story
Paolo Parente & Davide Fabbri — art
John Costanza — letters
Davide Fabbri, David Stewart, Jason Hvam, John Hanan III,
Geneva Smith & Brian Gregory — colour
Dave Chipps — editor

"Brute Creations"

Jan Strnad — story
Tommy Lee Edwards — pencils
Robert Campanella — inks
John Workman — letters
Melissa Edwards — colour
Dave Chipps — editor

"Starship Troopers"

Bruce Jones — story
Mitch Byrd — pencils
Andrew Pepoy — inks
Art Adams — art assist
Sean Konot — letters
Jim Brown — colour
Dave Chipps & Phil Amara — editor

BIG AND SMALL SCREEN CLASSICS FROM TITAN BOOKS

TO ORDER TELEPHONE 01536 763 631

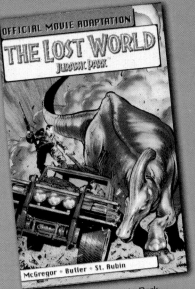

The Lost World: Jurassic Park
ISBN: 1 85286 885 6

Babylon 5
ISBN: 1 85286 646 2

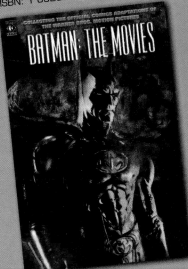

Batman: The Movies
ISBN: 1 85286 855 4

Babylon 5: Shadows Past and Present
ISBN: 1 85286 735 3

Space Above and Beyond
ISBN: 1 85286 771 X

The Lost World: Jurassic Park ™ & © 1997 Universal City Studios, Inc & Amblin Entertainment, Inc. Batman © 1997 DC Comics. Space Above and Beyond ™ & © 1997 Twentieth Century Fox Film Corporation. Babylon 5 © 1997 Warner Bros., a division of Time Warner Entertainment Company.